With an afterword by
BOBBY ORR

THE BOY in NUMBER FOUR

By **KARA KOOTSTRA** · Illustrated by **REGAN THOMSON**

Dial Books for Young Readers an imprint of Penguin Group (USA) LLC

In the ice rink locker room sat
the boy in Number Four,
lacing up his skates like so
many times before.

He thought of all his practices,
some early and some late.

The drills that he would
do to help him . . .

pass

and shoot

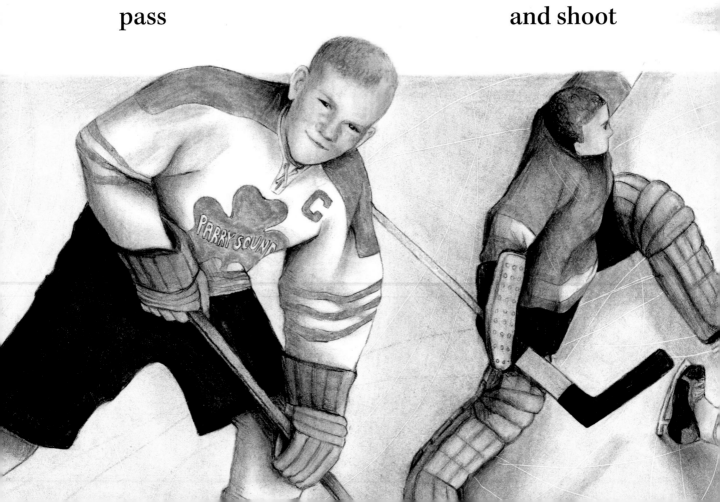

and skate.

There were times when it was easy,
and others that were tough,
but even when it seemed too hard,
he would never give up.

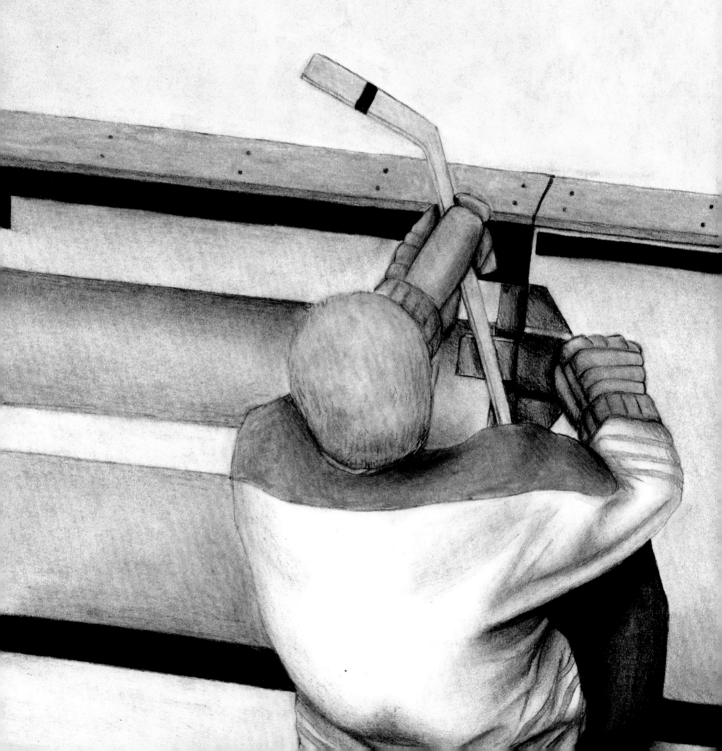

He'd sometimes get an injury,
a broken bone or bruise,

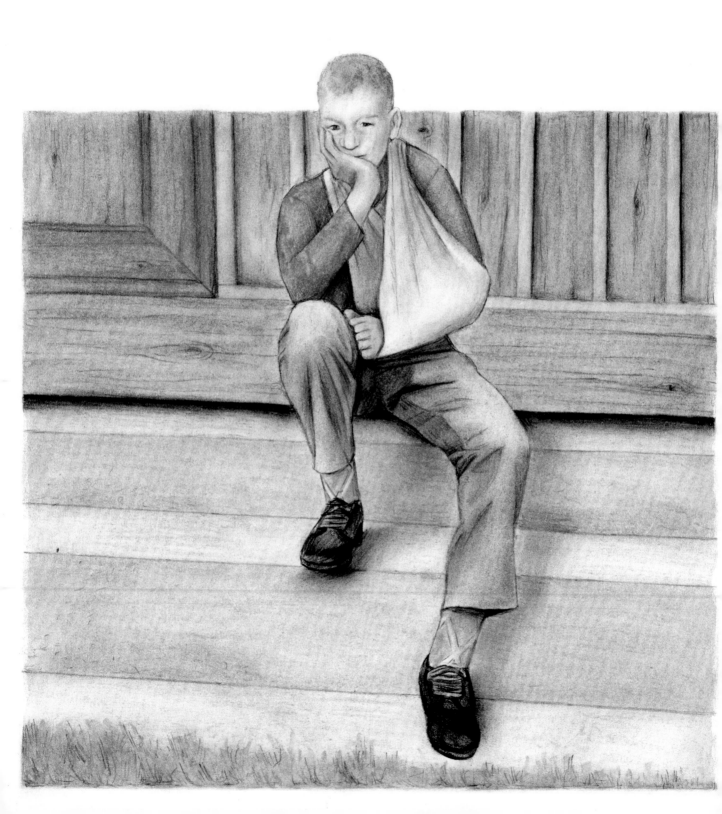

and though they did try hard to win,
sometimes his team would lose.

But the boy in Number Four
had a passion and a dream . . .
to one day be a player on a
big league hockey team!

Passing, shooting,
skating, his coaches
led the way,

and taught him to respect
both teams when it
was time to play.

For months and months
he'd practiced.
Now the game was
due to start . . .

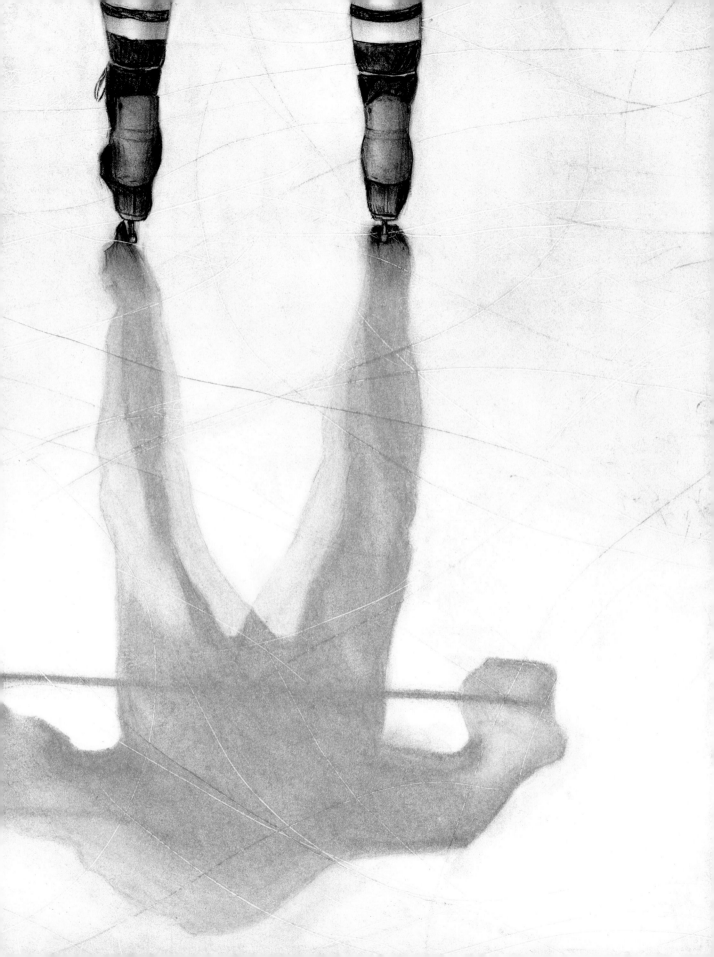

he skated out
before the crowd,
excitement in
his heart.

The whistle blows, the puck is dropped,
and off speeds Number Four,

passing,

shooting,

skating,
like so many times
before.

He sweeps around behind the net and up the ice
he races, his skate blades flash from left to right
in front of cheering faces.

Another player passes—now the puck is Number Four's.

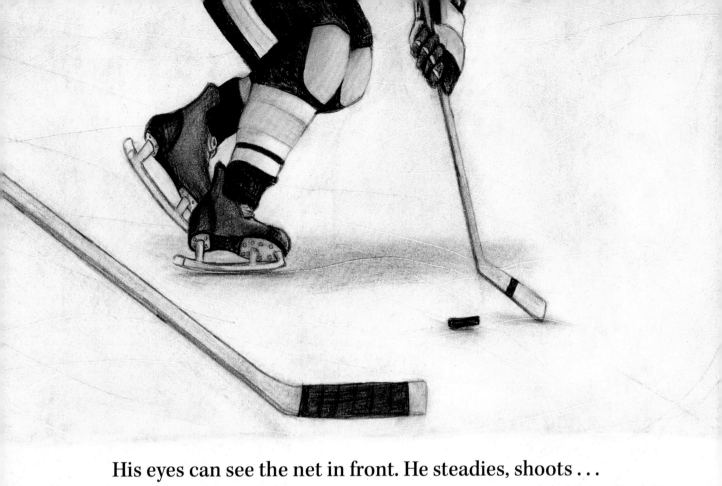

His eyes can see the net in front. He steadies, shoots . . .

he scores!

It's a goal for Number Four!

A game-winning goal for the amazing

Bobby Orr!

Afterword by
BOBBY ORR

When I was growing up, hockey was a very important part of my world. During the winter months my friends and I would play anywhere we could find ice—on Georgian Bay or the Seguin River or at a schoolyard rink. It really didn't matter where. As long as we could play hockey we were happy. I'd leave in the morning with my hockey stick and skates slung over my shoulder, and often my parents would say no more than "be home by dark." Sometimes we kept score, sometimes we didn't, but mostly our games were about the sheer joy of play, of being able to go outside with your buddies and simply have a good time. In those days, we didn't wait for an adult to organize our social time or sports experiences. We took that upon ourselves. We were the ones who decided when to get together, which game to play, and who would be on whose team. I'm a firm believer in kids just getting out and playing any kind of sport. Being part of a team, official or otherwise, should not just be an experience for the elite player. It should be something every child has a chance to experience.

The paintings in this book are based in large part on photos of me, growing up playing hockey. I learned a lot during all those years, honing the techniques and skills that would allow me to play against grown men while I was still a young teen. But most importantly, I learned respect—for the game itself and for everyone involved in it: my parents, who supported me throughout my childhood and career, my teammates and coaches, and members of opposing teams as well.

Today, thousands of kids growing up all around the world may be dreaming about making it to the NHL, and some may even succeed. But for everyone who loves hockey—young or old, player or spectator—I hope this book inspires you to simply pick up a stick, get together with some friends, and just have some fun playing the best game on earth.

To my father, Vern, the coach;

my husband, Kyle, my teammate;

and to Nate and Claire, my biggest fans.

—K.K.

To my husband, Steve, and my five children who are the best

support team and inspiration that this mom could ask for.

—R.T.

DIAL BOOKS FOR YOUNG READERS
Published by the Penguin Group
Penguin Group (USA) LLC
375 Hudson Street
New York, New York 10014

USA / Canada / UK / Ireland / Australia / New Zealand / India / South Africa / China
penguin.com
A Penguin Random House Company

Text copyright © 2014 by Kara Kootstra
Pictures copyright © 2014 by Regan Thomson
Afterword copyright © 2014 by Bobby Orr

Library of Congress Cataloging-in-Publication Data • Kootstra, Kara. • The boy in number four / written by Kara Kootstra ; pictures by Regan Thomson ; with an afterword by Bobby Orr. • pages cm • Summary: Young Bobby Orr works hard to be the best hockey player he can be and his efforts pay off in one of the many important games that help prepare him to achieve his dream of one day playing in the big leagues. • ISBN 978-0-8037-4167-6 (hardcover) • 1. Orr, Bobby, 1948—Childhood and youth—Juvenile fiction. [1. Stories in rhyme. 2. Orr, Bobby, 1948—Childhood and youth—Fiction. 3. Hockey—Fiction.] I. Thomson, Regan, illustrator. II. Title. • PZ8.3.K8427Boy 2014 • [E]—dc23 • 2013049843

Manufactured in China on acid-free paper
1 3 5 7 9 10 8 6 4 2
Type set in Kepler Std
Special Markets ISBN 978-0-5254-2944-9 Not for resale

Illustration pages 18–19 based on photograph copyright L'Agence France-Presse (AFP)
Illustration page 22 based on photograph copyright Courtney Szto
Illustration pages 28–29 based on photograph copyright the *Boston Herald*